I, *Geronimo Stilton*, have a
lot of mouse friends, but none
spooky as my friend CREEPELLA
VON CACKLEFUR! She is an
enchanting and MYSTERIOUS mouse with
a pet bat named **Bitewing**. Creepella lives in a
CEMETERY, sleeps in a marble **sarcophagus**, and drives
a **hearse**. By night she is a special effects and set
designer for SCARY FILMS, and by day she's studying
to become a journalist! Her father, Boris von
Cacklefur, runs the funeral home Fabumouse
Funerals, and the von Cacklefur family owns the
CREEPY Cacklefur Castle, which sits on top of a
skull-shaped mountain in MYSTERIOUS VALLEY.

YIKES! I'm a real 'fraidy
mouse, but even I think
Creepella and her family are
AWFULLY fascinating.
I can't wait for you to read
this **fa-mouse-ly funny** and
SPECTACULARLY SPOOKY tale!

Geronimo Stilton

Creepella von Cacklefur

Bitewing

Billy Squeakspeare

Grandpa Frankenstein

An extremely mad scientist and an expert in Egyptian mummies.

A journalist who lives in Mysterious Valley and solves spooky cases with her inseparable pet bat, Bitewing.

A famous writer and friend of Creepella.

Shivereen

Grandma Crypt

Snip and Snap

Troublemaking twins and expert spies.

Creepella's favorite niece.

Dolores

Kafka

She loves spiders, and her pet is a gigantic tarantula named Dolores.

The von Cacklefur family's pet cockroach.

Booey the Poltergeist

The mischievous ghost who haunts Cacklefur Castle.

Boneham

The butler to the von Cacklefur family, and a snob right down to the tips of his whiskers.

Baby

He was adopted and raised with love by the von Cacklefurs.

Chef Stewrat

The cook at Cacklefur Castle. He dreams of creating the ultimate stew.

Boris von Cacklefur

Creepella's father, and the funeral director at Fabumouse Funerals.

Madame LaTomb

The family housekeeper. A ferocious were-canary nests in her hair.

Chompers

The von Cacklefur family's meat-eating guard plant.

Geronimo Stilton

CREEPELLA VON CACKLEFUR

FRIGHT NIGHT

Scholastic Inc.

ISBN 978-0-545-39349-2

Based on an original idea by Elisabetta Dami.
www.geronimostilton.com

Published by Scholastic Inc., 557 Broadway, New York, NY 10012.
SCHOLASTIC and associated logos are trademarks and/or registered trademarks of Scholastic Inc.

Stilton is the name of a famous English cheese. It is a registered trademark of the Stilton Cheese Makers' Association. For more information, go to www.stiltoncheese.com.

Text by Geronimo Stilton
Original title *Il rap della paura*
Cover by Giuseppe Ferrario (pencils and inks) and Giulia Zaffaroni (color)
Illustrations by Ivan Bigarella (pencils and inks) and
Daria Cerchi (color)
Graphics by Yuko Egusa

Special thanks to Tracey West
Translated by Lidia Morson Tramontozzi
Interior design by Elizabeth Frances Herzog

12 11   17 18/0

Printed in the U.S.A.   40

First printing, June 2013

An Afternoon in the Library

A ray of sun as **yellow** as cheese sauce streamed through the window and lit up the rows and rows of **books** around me. The multicolored spines **glimmered** in the sunlight. I breathed deeply, enjoying the *lovely* smell of all that printed paper.

I'm sorry, I forgot to introduce myself. My name is Stilton, *Geronimo Stilton*. I'm the editor of *The Rodent's Gazette*, the most **FaMouse** newspaper on Mouse Island.

I was spending a pleasant afternoon in the **New Mouse City Library**. My nephew Benjamin was writing a research paper on ANCIENT Greece. I was happy to go with him because I had some work of my own to do. I had to read some documents about GLOOMERIA, the city where my friend CREEPELLA VON CACKLEFUR lives.

Why was I doing that, you ask? Her friend, the famouse author Billy Squeakspeare, had to leave for a LOOONG trip. So I had been helping Creepella put together a 754-volume encyclopedia about the GHOSTS of Gloomeria. Each volume is three thousand pages long. Yikes! Poor me!

As the sun began to set outside, it cast strange SHADOWS on the library floor. I put down the SPOOKY book about ghosts that I was reading and shivered. I needed a break!

I stretched and walked over to Benjamin's table. He looked up when he saw me.

"The ANCIENT Greeks were MOUSE-TASTIC!" he said.

I nodded. I found them fascinating, too.

"Did you know that they invented the theater?" Benjamin asked, his whiskers twitching with excitement. "They had these festivals where poets would compete to see who was the best."

"That sounds just like the FRIGHT NIGHT contest in Gloomeria!" I cried. "I was just reading about its history."

"Sssssssh!" grumbled a little gray mouse sitting at the table. Her snout was buried in a book called STINKY CHEESES AND THE RODENTS WHO LOVE THEM.

I ignored her and went to the bookshelf to find the book about the Fright Night contest. I was about to grab it when I noticed a TINY PAW on top of the book.

Then two **BEADY EYES** blinked at me over the book cover. "AAAAAAAAAAAAAHHH!"

I screamed. Then I realized that it was Bitewing, the pet bat of the von Cacklefur family.

"Why are you SHOUTING?" asked the cheeky little bat. "This is a library, not a football stadium!"

Wh-what do you want?

"What are you doing here?" I whispered. He handed me a **NOTEBOOK**

that he'd been clutching in his claws.

"**CREEPELLA** sent you this," he replied. "It's her new book. Publish it now! **No excuses!**"

Bitewing flew off and left me there TREMBLING. Had it just been a dream? But I held the **NOTEBOOK** in my 🐾🐾🐾🐾, which proved that I was awake!

Benjamin came over and took the book from me. He sat down to read it, and I looked over his shoulder. I started to shiver again. The book told the story of what had happened the last time I visited Creepella in Mysterious

Valley. It had been a truly **TERRIFYING** time . . . and I wasn't sure I wanted to remember it!

But the book was MOUSE-TATC, and I couldn't stop reading it. It was **DARK** when Benjamin and I finished.

As we walked home, we talked about the incredibly strange and Mysterious story we had just read.

"It's an awesome story, Uncle!" Benjamin said.

"You should publish it right away. **No excuses!**"

I had to admit that he was right. Even though the whole experience had given me nightmares, I couldn't keep this fantastic tale from Creepella's fans. So I published it! It's called **FRIGHT NIGHT**, and I'm sure you'll like it, too.

Happy reading!

FRIGHT NIGHT

STORY AND ILLUSTRATIONS BY
CREEPELLA VON CACKLEFUR

An Urgent Telegram

"Urgent TELEGRAM for Boris von Cacklefur!"

CREEPELLA VON CACKLEFUR and her niece Shivereen heard the cry. They ran outside as Cary Speedpaws, the mailmouse, rode up on

Thank you!

Here you go!

his bicycle. He handed a yellow sheet of paper to Creepella.

She read the note out loud:

URGENT MESSAGE!!!

DELIVER TO
BORIS VON CACKLEFUR, POET

"What is it? What is it? What is it?" Bitewing screeched.

Creepella smiled. "I think I know. But it's for Dad. Let's **hurry** and find him! He must be holed up someplace writing one of his poems."

"Maybe he's feeding his ALLIGATORS," Shivereen guessed. "He says they give him inspiration."

That's exactly where they found him — feeding little balls of Chef Stewrat's **Stinky Stew** to the alligators they kept in the castle.

There he is!

I love to rhyme all the time!

Every time he threw a ball of stew he made a rhyme.

"Here is some stew!
As you gnaw and chew,
I'll rhyme for you.
It's what I do!"

"Father, a telegram arrived for you," said Creepella, her **green** eyes gleaming.

Boris was surprised. "For me?"

"Read it! Read it! Read it!"

screeched Bitewing impatiently.

Curious, Boris silently read the telegram. Then he let out a cry, as though he had just been bitten by a **tarantula**.

"Rattle my bones!" he shouted. "This says that I'm a finalist in the **FRIGHT NIGHT** contest. But that's **impossible**. I didn't enter!"

"No, but I entered for you!" Creepella said.

The rest of the von Cacklefur family heard Boris's cry and started streaming into the room.

"What is all this **SHOUTING** about?" asked Madame LaTomb, the family's housekeeper.

"Whatever happened, it wasn't our fault!" said Snip and Snap, the **mischievous** twins.

"Not *this* time!" chirped Howler, the **ferocious** canary that lives in Madame LaTomb's hair.

"Our very own Boris is a finalist in the Fright Night contest!" Creepella announced. Everyone cheered, but Boris looked **gloomy**.

Hee hee hee!

"What's wrong, Father?" Creepella asked.

"I love to write **poetry**, but the last time I entered a competition it was truly **HORRIBLE**," her father answered. "I was a young ratling, in the fourth grade. I wrote a magnificent poem about graveyard **MOLD**. And then my classmate, Chester Cheater, stole the poem from my desk! I was so **upset** that I ran away. Chester won, and I was **heartbroken**. I vowed never to enter a poetry contest again."

"But your poems are too good to keep **hidden** away!" Creepella said. "That's why I entered you. You must share them with all of Mysterious Valley."

Boris sighed. "I suppose that was a long time ago. And I do have some delightfully **FRIGHTENING** new poems I'd like to share. . . ."

"Then it's settled!" Creepella said. "Now let's **HURRY**. The finals are today at **Horrorwood Studios**."

Creepella dashed outside to her **SUPERFAST** car, the **Turborapid 3000**. Boris, Shivereen, and Bitewing followed her.

"On the way, I'll pick up *Geronimo Stilton*," Creepella said. "He's staying at Squeakspeare Mansion, working on the ENCYCLOPEDIA."

When they arrived at the MANSION, Geronimo was in the garden.

Sigh . . .

He held a telegram between his paws, and he looked miserable.

"You received a telegram, too?" Shivereen asked.

Geronimo handed it to Creepella.

CONGRATULATIONS!

YOU HAVE BEEN SELECTED AS
AN OFFICIAL JUDGE
FOR THE FRIGHT NIGHT CONTEST!
REPORT IMMEDIATELY TO HORRORWOOD STUDIOS . . .
OR ELSE!

"You're so **LUCKY**, Gerrykins!" Creepella exclaimed.

Geronimo frowned. "Lucky? Fright Night? I'm too *BUSY* to be a judge. I'm working on the encyclopedia of GHOSTS, remember?"

"No excuses!" Creepella said firmly. "This is a real honor. And I'm going to write a *fantastic* article about the whole thing!"

THE SHIVERS
MACHINE

Creepella pushed Geronimo into her car and sped off.

"I'm so **curious**!" she said. "Every year, Spruce Dazzlefur, the set director, creates a **spectacular** set for the contest. I wonder what he'll do this year?"

They quickly arrived at the studios and followed the signs to the Fright Night arena. A stage shaped like a **HALF** oval looked like it was inspired by ancient Greece. **GLOOMY** drapes formed the backdrops. **FRIGHT NIGHT** fans were beginning to fill the stands that surrounded the stage.

"*Awesome!* This year Dazzlefur outdid himself!" Shivereen exclaimed as she looked around.

Geronimo was looking around, too — for a way to *escape*. He wanted to get back to work. He still had thousands of pages to write.

But a **STRONG** paw slapped him on the shoulder.

"**CHEESE AND CRACKERS!** If it isn't the most famouse writer from New Mouse City! Our final judge!"

It was Professor Dubloon, who teaches **Pirate History** at the Academy of Arts and Shivers. He lifted his **eyepatch** and winked at Creepella.

We're all here!

Beautiful!

"Hello, Professor!" Creepella said. "Are you a **judge**, just like my little Gerrykins?"

"That's right," Dubloon answered. "Along with your former TEACHER, Professor Cleverpaws. And a rather BORING reporter from *The Gloomeria Times*. I'm sure even the SHIVERS MACHINE won't wake her up!"

Geronimo's **ears** perked up. "Sh-shivers Machine?" he asked.

Creepella pointed to the judges' table. Each of the four seats had a *rope* tied to it. And the ropes were tied to a strange-looking **purple casket**.

"That's it," she explained. "When the judges get SCARED, they will **shake** and

SHIVER, making the ropes tremble. The shivers get recorded by the machine, which lights up in colors ranging from **PUTRID PURPLE** to FULL-MOON WHITE. It goes all the way from 'Slightly Spooked' to 'Fainting from Fright.'"

"Why, exactly, would the judges get **SCARED**?" Geronimo wondered.

"Don't you know, Gerrykins?" Creepella asked. "That's the whole purpose of the contest. The winning poet is the one who can frighten the judges the most!"

Geronimo turned as PALE as a slice of mozzarella just thinking about what was in store.

"You're the same

color as the SHIVERS MACHINE!" Bitewing exclaimed.

Geronimo tried to run for the exit again, but this time Professor Cleverpaws stopped him.

"If it isn't the most FAMOUSE writer in New Mouse City!" she said. "How nice to meet you! We must sit down. The competition is about to begin."

Come, let's sit down!

I should be going. . . . .

LET THE CONTEST BEGIN!

Professor Cleverpaws *pushed* Geronimo toward the judges' table. Professor Dubloon was already seated next to a rodent with gray fur who was fast **asleep**.

"That's Evelyn Dozer, the OLDEST reporter at *The Gloomeria Times*," Professor Cleverpaws **explained**. "She is head of the Obituaries department."

"Nice to meet you," Geronimo said politely.

Professor Cleverpaws coughed lightly. "Ahem . . . she won't answer. She's been **sleeping** for more than six years."

Geronimo reluctantly took a seat next to Professor Dubloon. An assistant appeared and began to tie his tail to the *rope* that was connected to the SHIVERS MACHINE.

Before Geronimo could protest, the host of the contest, Crystal Glamorosa, appeared on the stage. She wore a **BLACK DRESS** with a cape that looked like bat wings.

"Hello Gloomeria!"

Crystal Glamorosa

she shouted, and the audience went **WILD**. "Welcome to Fright Night, the contest to find the most terrifying poet in all of Mysterious Valley!"

The fans CLAPPED, **cheered**, and **HOOTED**.

Then Crystal explained the rules of the contest.

"**FOUR** talented poets are here today, but only **TWO** will make it to the finals," she said. "The last poet standing will earn the DISTINGUISHED title of

FRIGHT NIGHT IDOL!"

The crowd burst into applause, filling the arena with a sound like *thunder*.

"The two poets who make it to the finals will each try to make the judges SHIVER the most," she went on. "The shivers can only be caused by their **PETRIFYING POEMS**. No shivering from **other** sources — such as fans or air conditioners — is allowed."

Then Crystal dramatically pointed to the curtain behind her.

"Allow me to present our talented contestants!"

VERA VERSA

she announced.

The curtain opened, revealing four rodents dressed in **PURPLE TUNICS**.

"First, a poet with a personality as thrilling as an earthworm, the deeply depressing **VERA VERSA!**"

In the front row, Vera's family let out a gloomy cheer. "**Whoooaaaaaahh!**" they moaned.

"Second, from the **DARK** and mysterious

Cacklefur castle, that fantastic funeral director,

BORIS VON CACKLEFUR!"

Creepella, Bitewing, and Shivereen cheered **wildly** from the sidelines.

Then Crystal pointed to the third contestant, a teenage mouse with **spiky**

black fur on her head.

"Our third poet is a young rodent with a truly gloomy outlook on life,

Lyrica Sonnetail!"

A group of teenage fans in the back row waved black-and-purple **POM-POMS**.

BORIS VON CACKLEFUR

Lyrica Sonnetail

"And finally, the **FRIGHT NIGHT IDOL** for six years running, the most horrifying poet in all of Mysterious Valley, our somber superstar, **Brad Balladeer**!"

The crowd **EXPLODED** as the famouse poet took a bow. The three rodents who cheered the loudest were those troublemaking triplets, the Rattenbaum sisters.

Brad Balladeer

"You're the best!"

"You're so handsome!"

"You're fabulous!"

Go, Brad!

You're so handsome!

You're the scariest!

Shamley, the triplets' grandfather, agreed. "And he's very HIGH-CLASS!" he added. "What a rat!"

Crystal opened her arms wide.

"Let the contest begin!"

ROUND ONE:
THE ROTTEN RAP

"I didn't realize Brad Balladeer was going to be here," said Shivereen **nervously**. "He's a tough competitor!"

Are you sure?

Creepella sniffed. "He gets by on **GLITZ** and good looks! His poems are completely unoriginal. Father will beat him easily."

"Are you sure?" Shivereen asked.

Creepella nodded. "I **PEEKED** in Father's notebook. His latest **poems** are truly **TERRIFYING**. One is a real masterpiece."

"What's it called?" asked her niece.

"**THE PHANTOM'S TALE**," Creepella whispered. "But don't tell anybody!"

Then Horatio Puffyfur, the Fright Night official, sat next to the SHIVERS MACHINE. It was his job to record the scores of each contestant.

Crystal spoke up again. "For the first round, each contestant will create a verse of a rap song on the spot," she announced. "It's time for **The Rotten Rap**!"

The crowd *oohed* and **aahed**.

"To get our poets started, we're lucky to have two of the top **RaPPinG RoDents** in all of Mysterious Valley," Crystal said. "Put your paws together for . . . **The Creepy Crew**!"

Creepella clapped. "What a **TREAT**! I love these two. Their rhymes are nauseating, and they have a great beat."

The sound of a **HEAVY** bass beat filled the arena. Then two **rappers** holding microphones bounded onto the stage — **MOUSE Z** and **SQUEAK RAT**, the Creepy Crew.

The rappers JUMPED up and down to the beat.

"Do you think Grandfather Boris can RAP?" Shivereen whispered.

"I'm not sure," Creepella replied. "Let's see what happens."

Then The Creepy Crew launched into the first verse of their rap:

On a dark and stormy night,
In the middle of the woods,
A young rodent was lost.
She was wearing a red hood.
Boom–ch–ch–Boom–ch–ch–Boom
Boom Boom

It was Vera Versa's turn next. She rapped in a high, shrill voice.

The rain poured down.
The young rat was a mess.
Her fur was very damp
And she had mud on her dress!
Boom–ch–ch–Boom–ch–ch–Boom
Boom Boom

The crowd applauded weakly, and the Shivers Machine didn't move at all. Then it was Boris's turn.

A wet, muddy dress
Is not much of a scare.
But look at those shadows —
I see something there!
Boom–ch–ch–Boom–ch–ch–Boom
Boom Boom

Then it was teenage mouse Lyrica Sonnetail's turn.

> The shadows were gloomy,
> and dark, and dreary.
> The girl became dismal,
> and solemn, and teary.
> Boom-ch-ch-Boom-ch-ch-Boom
> Boom Boom

The Shivers Machine was starting to move. All eyes turned to Brad Balladeer, to see what the master poet would do. He spoke in a loud, commanding voice.

> Then a ghost cat jumped out!
> The young rat let out a scream.
> The ghost twirled about.
> The end. I am supreme!
> Boom-ch-ch-Boom-ch-ch-Boom
> Boom Boom

ROUND TWO: MIND-BENDING RIDDLES

The **crowd** clapped and the Creepy Crew left the stage. Horatio Puffyfur gave the results of the SHIVERS MACHINE.

"Brad Balladeer gets fifteen points. Boris von Cacklefur earns ten points. Lyrica Sonnetail earns five points, and Vera Versa earns zero," he announced.

The Rattenbaum triplets cheered **wildly** for Brad, but Creepella wasn't worried.

"This isn't over yet," she told Shivereen.

Then the stage began to **tremble**, and four **skull-shaped** booths rose up from the floor.

"OOOOOOOOOOOOOOHHHHHHH!"

The crowd was truly amazed.

"Contestants, please enter a booth," Crystal instructed. "In this round, you will each be asked to solve a **MIND-BENDING RIDDLE** after hearing three clues. If you guess correctly you will earn ten points. From here on out, the poet with the lowest score at the end of each round will be **ELIMINATED!**"

"My father should do very well," Creepella whispered to Shivereen. "He can solve a riddle faster than a spider can spin a web!"

Crystal opened an envelope. "**BORIS VON CACKLEFUR**, you're up first. Here is your first **CLUE**: The mouse who **makes** this doesn't need it."

Boris nodded but didn't answer.

"Second **CLUE**: The mouse who **buys** it will not use it."

Boris smiled and waited for the next clue.

"Third 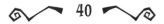: The mouse who **uses** it will never see it! What is it?"

Boris looked confident. "It's a **COFFIN**, of course!"

Creepella clapped happily. "Great job, Dad!"

It was Brad's turn next. The famouse poet closed his eyes, concentrating.

"First , Brad: You cannot t◕◡c♥ it, hear it, or smell it, but you know when it is around you."

Brad opened one eye, but did not answer.

"Second **CLUE**: It can fill **H◉LES**, but it has no shape."

Brad didn't wait for the third clue. He raised his arms triumphantly.

"It's **DARKNESS**, obviously!"

The crowd went **wild**. Then it was Vera Versa's turn. She was as pale as mozzarella.

"Vera, here is your first **CLUE**," Crystal began. "It has no **VOICE**, but you can hear it cry."

Vera waited for the second **CLUE**.

"It can **tear apart** trees, but it has no arms."

The crowd was rumbling. Many had guessed the answer, but not Vera.

"Third **CLUE**: You can **feel** it, but you can't see it."

Vera's eyes suddenly lit up. "Is it the *wind*?"

"**Correct**!" Crystal cried, and everyone clapped.

It was Lyrica's turn. The mouselet looked like she was getting extremely *bored* with the whole contest. Crystal started to read the first **CLUE**.

"It's as **BLACK** as . . ."

"It's a **DARK NIGHT** without a moon!" Lyrica answered impatiently.

Crystal shook her head. "I'm sorry. The right answer was . . . a crow! Lyrica, since the round is over and you only have five points, you are **ELIMINATED!**"

Then the stage opened up, and Lyrica's booth quickly **DISAPPEARED** beneath it.

ROUND THREE:
TERROR TIME

"Grandfather Boris is still in the game," said Shivereen. "And to think, he didn't even want to enter!"

"I *know* he can **WIN**," Creepella said confidently. "No one can **rhyme** like Boris von Cacklefur."

At the judges' table, Professor Dubloon **eagerly** rubbed his paws together.

"It's about to get **REALLY SCARY**," he said, nudging Geronimo, whose whiskers began to twitch nervously. "We may even see our sleeping reporter **WAKE UP**!"

Crystal Glamorosa faced the audience once more.

"Now it's time for **Round Three!**" she declared. "It's **TERROR TIME**! Each contestant will be assigned one word. Then they'll have exactly one minute to compose a **BLOOD-CURDLING** poem based on the word!"

"A minute is not much time," Shivereen remarked.

"Brad, since you're in the lead, you go first," Crystal said. She pointed to Horatio Puffyfur, who held up FOUR ENVELOPES. "Pick a number from one to four, Brad."

"**NUMBER THREE!**" said the poet dramatically.

Crystal took the envelope from Horatio and read the word out loud.

"Tomb!"

The arena was SILENT as Horatio counted a minute on his stopwatch. Then he nodded to Brad, who began his poem confidently.

"I slowly walked inside the tomb.
Among the spiderwebs and bones.
It was a dark and dreary room,
And I was cold and all alone.
Then suddenly, my light went out,
And the skulls began to scream and shout!"

"TRULY TERRIFYING!"

shouted the audience members.

Marvelous!

Terrific!

Bravo!

The best!

The Shivers Machine went all the way up to "Fainting from Fright." Geronimo was so scared he tried to **run away**, but the rope was tied to his tail, and he **TRIPPED** and fell!

Oops!

"That ~~TERRIFYING~~ rhyme will be tough to beat!" said Crystal. She looked at Boris. "All right, Boris, it's your turn. Choose an envelope!"

"**NUMBER ONE**!" Boris said, and then Crystal read the word.

"Grave!"

"Dad should be able to ace this one," Creepella whispered to Shivereen.

Boris closed his eyes, ~~thinking~~, as the minute clicked away. Then Horatio gave him the signal to start.

"I WANDERED PAST A GHASTLY GRAVE,
AND SAW THE DIRT HAD BEEN MOVED ABOUT.
BEFORE I COULD RUN, OR EVEN SCREAM,
A BONY SKELETON JUMPED RIGHT OUT!"

The arrow on the Shivers Machine jumped nearly all the way to the top, to the "**POSITIVELY PETRIFYING**" level. Creepella and Shivereen let out a cheer.

The audience liked the poem, too.

"Frightfully chilling!"

"A real stomach-turner!"

Boris smiled, pleased. Then it was Vera Versa's turn. She chose number four, and Crystal shouted her word:

"Phantom!"

After a minute, Vera began:

"A phantom sat down to breakfast.
It was the meal he liked the most.
But he had no bread, so the phantom said,
'I'm a ghost without any toast!'"

The audience was SILENT at first. Then they began to laugh. Then the judges laughed. Crystal and Horatio laughed. The only rodents who weren't laughing were Evelyn Dozer, who was still asleep, and Vera Versa, who knew that she had lost. The Shivers Machine arrow was moving — but from laughter, not from fright.

Crystal delivered the verdict.

"ELIMINATED!" she cried.

Poof! Vera Versa's booth disappeared beneath the stage. Crystal dried her TEARS (from laughing so hard) and then announced, "The final two **FRIGHT NIGHT** contestants are Brad Balladeer and Boris von Cacklefur!"

"Brad! Brad!"

cheered half the crowd.

"BORIS! BORIS!"

cheered the other half.

Crystal waved to the audience. "It's time for intermission! We'll be back in twenty minutes!"

Boris left the stage and joined Creepella and Shivereen.

"You're doing GREAT, Father!" Creepella said, giving him a hug.

"Thank you," Boris replied. "But Brad is going to be difficult to beat. And there's something ODDLY familiar about him. . . ." He thoughtfully pulled his whiskers.

"You'd better start practicing your final poem, Father," Creepella reminded him.

"Yes, OF COURSE!" Boris agreed. Then he walked off to his dressing room.

Bye-bye!

See you later!

Bravo!

THREE SUSPICIOUS THINGS

Geronimo slowly untied the *rope* from his tail. Professor Dubloon was busy chatting with Professor Cleverpaws. Evelyn Dozer was **snoring** away next to him. It was the perfect time to **ESCAPE**!

"They don't really need me," he reasoned. "I need to get back to my writing."

He **SLOWLY** began to tiptoe away. Then he **scurried** backstage, where he hoped he wouldn't be seen. To his **SURPRISE**, he found Brad Balladeer talking with the Rattenbaum triplets. All four were clutching long **BANDAGES** in their paws.

"He's the perfect mummy!" Brad told the triplets, laughing.

Geronimo forgot all about his escape plan. There was something SUSPICIOUS about this scene.

"What mummy are you talking about?" he asked them. "And why do you need all these bandages?"

It was so easy!

What fun!

Tee hee!

Great work, my dears!

"Oh, look, it's Creepella's friend," said Lilly.

"Why do you hang around with her?" asked Milly.

"We're much more interesting," said Tilly.

Before Geronimo could respond, Brad stepped up to him. "I asked these lovely ladies to help inspire me," he said. "I need a rhyme for my poem, 'Ode to the Mummy.' The bandages help get me in a mummy mood."

"Bandages? Really?" asked Geronimo.

Brad rolled his eyes impatiently. Then he turned to the Rattenbaums. "Let us go, my muses. Poetry does not wait!"

What do you mean?

Geronimo watched them head toward Brad's dressing room. He didn't believe their story, but he had other things to think about.

"I must go work on that **ENCYCLOPEDIA**!" he said. "The faster I finish, the faster I can get away from this **BIZARRE** valley!"

He was only a few steps away from the back door when he heard **CREEPELLA'S** voice behind him.

"Here you are, Gerrykins!" she said. "I've been looking for you!"

Geronimo turned and saw Creepella holding a pot of **STEAMING** stew.

"Isn't it wonderful? Chef Stewrat and the whole von Cacklefur family are here," she said. "A pot of Chef's stew is just the thing to give Father the **ENERGY** he needs to win. Would you like some?"

Geronimo sniffed at the stinky stew and then shook his head.

"Well, come anyway," she said. "I'm sure Father can use some encouragement."

"B-but the encyclopedia . . ." Geronimo stammered.

Then he felt a paw on his back.

"YOU DID IT! I KNOW YOU DID! CONFESS!"

It was Professor Dubloon. Geromino was very **CONFUSED**.

"By the strings of my **eyepatch**, it was you!" the angry professor went on. "You **thief!**"

"What happened?" Creepella asked gently.

"Somebody **STOLE** my ship!" Dubloon roared. "It was parked right outside the arena. And now it's **GONE!**"

"Your ship?" asked Geronimo.

"The professor has a pirate ship on **wheels**," Creepella explained. "I wonder who would want to steal it?"

Dubloon pointed at Geronimo.

"HE STOLE IT!"

"Don't be **SILLY**, Professor!" Creepella said with a laugh. "Geronimo is the most *honest* rodent I know. We'll help you later. We need to go see my father!"

Creepella **grabbed**

It was you!

You're wrong!

Hee hee!

Geronimo by the elbow and led him to Boris's dressing room. But when she opened the door, she was SURPRISED to find that her father wasn't there.

"Where could he be?" Creepella asked.

"Hmm," muttered Geronimo to himself. "A mysterious mummy. A missing vehicle. And now this. It's all very SUSPICIOUS."

Just then the Rattenbaum triplets walked past the door, snickering.

He's not here!

Tee hee!

WHERE'S BORIS?

When they saw Creepella, the triplets stopped laughing.

"Look who's here!" said Milly.

"It's boring old Creepella," added Tilly.

"I bet she's looking for her daddy," sneered Lilly.

Creepella marched up to them.

"How do you know that?" she asked. "Have you seen my father?"

"Your father is a SCAREDY-RAT," Milly said.

"He knew that Brad is going to WIN," said Tilly.

"So he RAN away!" Lilly finished.

"He would NeVeR do that!" Creepella insisted.

"Oh, no? That's what he did in fourth grade," the triplets said together.

Creepella's green eyes flashed with anger. "How did you know that?"

But the triplets HURRIED away without answering. Creepella started to go after them, but Geronimo held her back.

"Calm down," he said. "I have something to tell you."

"Not now, Geronimo," Creepella said **impatiently**. "We must find Father!"

Creepella ran so fast that Geronimo could not keep up. She found her family in the stands. They were enjoying Chef Stewrat's smelly stew.

"Father is MISSING!" Creepella announced. "The Rattenbaum triplets said he ran away, but I don't believe them!"

"Well, he *was* nervous about the contest," Shivereen pointed out.

"True, but he is very PROUD of that poem he wrote," Creepella said. "I know he wants to recite it in the final round."

"Maybe that Brad Balladeer fellow knows something," muttered Grandma Crypt. "That young rat looks quite familiar. . . ."

Geronimo finally caught up to Creepella.

"I have something to tell you," he told her, huffing and puffing. "It's important!"

Whaaaat?

He's really gone!

He's not here!

Pant . . .

"Father is missing," Creepella said. "That's more important!"

"But I think something SUSPICIOUS is going on," Geronimo insisted. "Before Boris went missing, I saw Brad with the Rattenbaum triplets and a bunch of bandages. They were acting very STRANGE."

"That is suspicious," Creepella said. "I think you're onto something, Gerrykins. Let's go solve this MYSTERY!"

They headed back to Boris's dressing room to look for CLUES. Shivereen, who always loved a good mystery, joined them. So did Bitewing, but he went along for the mosquito treats in Creepella's pockets.

As they walked down the hall, they saw Professor Cleverpaws examining the floor with a huge magnifying glass.

"Professor, are you looking for my father, too?" Creepella asked.

"Your father? I didn't know he was missing," the professor replied. "No, I'm trying to help Professor Dubloon find his missing **pirate ship**."

"That's another **suspicious** disappearance," Geronimo remarked.

Creepella nodded. "Exactly! And I have a hunch that those two disappearances are connected. If we **find** the pirate ship, we'll **find** Father!"

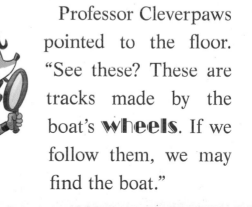

Professor Cleverpaws pointed to the floor. "See these? These are tracks made by the boat's **wheels**. If we follow them, we may find the boat."

Everyone eagerly followed Professor Cleverpaws as she moved along the **tracks**, but then she stopped at the entrance to the **Horrorwood Studios** gate. Beyond the gate were the sets for the movies made at the studio.

"There are too many **tracks** beyond the gate," the professor said, shaking her head. "I'll have to **STOP** following them."

"Don't worry, we'll take it from here!" Creepella promised.

"But we don't even know where to look," Geronimo **protested**. "This could take **FOREVER**."

Creepella ignored him and **PUSHED** open the gate. Shivereen and Bitewing followed her, and Geronimo reluctantly joined them.

Next to the gate, three blonde heads poked

out of three large fake rocks.

"She's getting too close," said Milly

"We have to follow her!" added Lilly.

"She can't find out what happened," warned Tilly.

A Busy Movie Set

The studio lot was **crowded** with rodents scurrying between the *BUSY* movie sets. As they began their search, Geronimo turned to Creepella.

"What did those **triplets** mean before?" he asked. "About your father in fourth grade?"

Creepella told him the story of how Chester Cheater **STOLE** young Boris's poem. "He never entered a contest again," she explained. "But that was a long time ago. I'm sure he hasn't *run away*!"

Then the Rattenbaum triplets strolled by, carrying S U I T C A S E S.

"We're carrying our costumes," said
Milly.

"We're going to be stars!" added
Lilly.

"Beauties of the big screen!" bragged
Tilly.

Then they HURRIED off.

It's them again!

We're going
to be stars!

Creepella's eyes narrowed. "I don't trust those three."

"What should we do now, Auntie?" Shivereen asked.

"Let's talk to my friend, the movie director SYLVIA CINEMOUSE," Creepella suggested. "Maybe she's seen something."

They found Sylvia on the set of her new film, FOREST OF FUR.

"Creepella, how good to see you!" she cried. "Can I convince you to STAR in my next film? I've got the PERFECT part for you."

Creepella shook her head.

"Thanks, but being an ACTRESS isn't in my plans."

"That's too bad," said Sylvia. "You've got a **GREAT** look, and a **GREAT** name, too."

"Name?" asked Shivereen.

"Sure," said Sylvia. "Every **MOVIE STAR** needs a great name. Take Johnny Depprat, the **FAMOUSE** actor. His name used to be Henry Squishyface. He never got any work. Then he changed it, and now he's a **STAR**!"

While Creepella and her friend talked, Geronimo looked around the set for clues. He **TRIPPED** over three bushes that seemed to come out of nowhere.

"How dare you, you **CLUMSY** rodent!" said the bushes. Then they shuffled away.

"**Quiet**, everyone!" Sylvia shouted through her megaphone. "This is a movie set."

"Sorry," Geronimo said. "But we're trying to solve a **MYSTERY** here. Creepella's father is missing."

"Oh, dear," said Sylvia. "How can I help?"

"We were wondering if you've seen a **pirate ship** on wheels roll through here," Creepella said.

Sylvia shook her head. "Sorry, no. It's been **CRAZY** around here all morning. But if I see one, I'll let you know."

Then Shivereen cried out in a **LOUD** voice.

"Auntie, come here! I think I've found something!"

Mysterious Fragments

Creepella ran to Shivereen, who was holding up a **TORN** scrap of paper.

"I found it on the ground, and there are some weird **TRACKS** right next to it," Shivereen reported. "It has one word on it: '**Once**.'"

"Hmm. Once," repeated Creepella.

Shivereen moved forward along the **TRACKS**.

"Hey, look! Here's another! And another!"

Once

Geronimo caught up to them, and they all worked together to pick up the **SCRAPS**

of paper. Each one had **WORDS** on it. Creepella started to rearrange them like a **PUZZLE**. Then she gasped.

"Rats and bats! This is —"

"What is it? What is it? What is it?" Bitewing interrupted.

"**Look!**" Creepella said urgently. "It's the first verse of my father's poem, **'THE PHANTOM'S TALE'**!"

> Once upon a midnight scary

"But why is the poem all **TORN** up?" Shivereen wondered. "And what are the pieces doing here?"

"This is an **IMPORTANT** clue," Creepella said.

Geronimo was walking with his head down, looking for more scraps of the poem, when he **BUMPED** into a rodent.

"Don't be so **CLUMSY!**" the rodent snapped.

"I'm sorry," Geronimo said. Then he looked up. "**Brad Balladeer**? What are you doing here?"

It's Father's poem!

A clue!

Awesome!

"I could ask you the same thing," Brad replied.

Creepella marched over. Her eyes narrowed *suspiciously*.

"Geronimo asked you first," she said. "What are you doing here?"

A **dark** look crossed Brad's face. "I'm just going on a little walk before the final round. Why? Is that against the rules?"

"No, it isn't," CREEPELLA answered

Oof!

Oops!

smoothly. "But that answer smells like a LIE to me!"

Brad sniffed, turned around quickly, and HURRIED away. As he left, Geronimo spotted something shiny on the ground.

"It's a watch," Geronimo said, picking it up. "With the letters 'C.C.' engraved on the back."

"That's strange," Creepella remarked. "Brad's initials are 'B.B.'"

Shivereen tugged at Creepella's sleeve. "Auntie, look!" she said, pointing at the floor. "Brad left some strange PAW PRINTS behind."

Creepella knelt down to examine them. "Rats and bats!" she exclaimed. "This is . . . SAND!"

DOWN BY THE SEA

"**Sand?**" asked Shivereen. "How did it get onto Brad's paws?"

"Easy!" Creepella replied. "It came from the **sea**!"

"The sea? But that's not anywhere near here," Geronimo pointed out.

"I'm obviously talking about a **MOVIE SET**, Gerrykins," Creepella said. She started to **HURRY** away. "We need to find out what Brad was doing around here. Then I'm sure we'll find the **SOLUTION** to our mystery!"

"Where are we going, Auntie?" Shivereen asked, hurrying after her.

"My friend Marco Megamouse is directing an **action movie** that takes place on an island," she replied. "There might be sand there."

They raced to the set. Marco JUMPED out of his chair when he saw Creepella.

"My friend, what **Ghastly Glamour** you possess!" he said. "You must star in my new film."

"I'm sorry," Creepella replied. "I don't have time. You see, I'm looking for —"

"We have the time!" Lilly Rattenbaum interrupted.

"We even have costumes!" Tilly said.

"We can be in your film!" Milly finished.

The Rattenbaum triplets had popped out from behind some plants, dressed as lobsters.

Marco eyed them. "Hmm. My MOVIE'S main character is a great detective. You could play his assistants. Climb up on those rocks over there."

The triplets **squealed** with delight and took their places on the set.

"I'm curious, what is this film about?" Shivereen asked Marco.

"It's called:

It's about that great sleuth, Squidlock Holmes," he replied.

"I hate to bother you, but we have a real problem," Creepella said. "My father is MISSING. We think he was whisked away in a **pirate ship** on wheels. The tracks led inside the studios. And a SUSPICIOUS character connected to the mystery has sand on his paws. Is there any sand on your set?"

"No, this is a ROCKY island," the director replied.

Creepella frowned. "This doesn't make sense. Where could Brad have gotten that SaND?"

Marco grabbed his **MEGAPHONE** and held it to his snout. "All right, everybody! **ACTION!**"

There was a loud roar, and a **Giant wave** rose from the fake ocean, soaking the Rattenbaums. Then an **ENORMOUSE tentacle** splashed out of the water, and another, and another . . . and then two **RED** eyes . . . and then a big, **slimy** body.

Geronimo promptly fainted from fright.

"Poor Gerrykins," Creepella said. "Everyone knows that Squidlock Holmes is a *giant squid*!"

83

"What an awesome squid!" Shivereen cheered. "Even if it is just movie magic."

The Rattenbaums were furious, and they took it out on Creepella.

"You're slimier than a spitting snake!"

"You're nastier than a cranky alligator!"

"You're mustier than an old mummy!"

You're a musty mummy!

You're a slimy snake!

It's your fault!

That's it!

THE TALKING SARCOPHAGUS

Creepella **RACED** off with Shivereen at her heels.

"A mummy!" repeated Creepella. "The SAND on Brad's paws didn't come from a beach. It came from a DESERT!"

"A desert?" asked Shivereen.

Creepella nodded. "The great Filmini, my favorite director, is making a movie about ancient EGYPT."

They found Filmini on a set surrounded by SAND, PYRAMIDS, and hundreds of SARCOPHAGI — ancient mummy cases. Creepella got right to the point.

"Did Brad Balladeer pass through here?"

The director nodded. "He was on a strange boat on **wheels**, together with three blonde triplets."

"The Rattenbaums!" hissed Creepella. "I knew those rats had a paw in this caper."

Shivereen pointed to the floor. "Look, Auntie. It's those same tracks, and another **SCRAP** of paper."

It was followed by an eerie sound.

Creepella was certain. "This is another line from Father's **poem**. Let's see if we can find any more."

Geronimo finally caught up to them. He was out of breath.

"The finals . . . *HUFF* . . . of the poetry contest . . . *PUFF* . . . are about to begin!"

Then Shivereen called out. "Auntie! Over here!"

She had found another scrap of paper behind a **pyramid**. Geronimo suddenly noticed the hundreds of sarcophagi and turned PALE.

"It's not real, Gerrykins; it's just a movie set," Creepella reminded him. "It's called

THE GREAT TUTANKAMOUSE."

Shivereen handed the newest scrap to Creepella, who nodded. "Yes, it's more of the poem. Something tells me that Father is around here somewhere!"

Suddenly, Geronimo began to **tremble** like a wobbly bowl of cottage cheese.

"Cr-creepella! That **sarcophagus** over there is m-moving!" he stammered.

"It's moving! It's moving! It's moving!"

shouted Bitewing.

Creepella and Shivereen ran to the sarcophagus. A muffled **SCREAM** came from inside.

"Get me **OUT** of here!"

"The sarcophagus is talking!" Geronimo cried.

"Of course! Father is inside," Creepella said. "Father, *can you hear me*?"

"CREEPELLA!" It was Boris's voice, all right. "You finally found me!"

"How did you end up in there?" Geronimo asked.

Inside the **sarcophagus**, Boris growled angrily. "It was no accident. I was **MOUSENAPPED!**"

Father?

MYSTERY SOLVED!

"Mousenapped! What an **AWFUL** thing!" Geronimo exclaimed.

"Yes," Creepella agreed. "And I know who did it, too. It was **Brad Balladeer**!"

"Exactly!" Boris cried. "That sneaky sewer rat is responsible for this! I was in my dressing room, rehearsing '**A PHANTOM'S TALE**,' when Brad burst in with those awful Rattenbaum sisters. They wrapped me up like a MUMMY and stuffed me in a sack!"

"How **TERRIBLE**, Grandfather!" Shivereen cried.

Creepella nodded. "And then they **STOLE**

Professor Dubloon's pirate ship on wheels and sped onto this set with you, right?"

"Right as always, my clever daughter," Boris replied. "They **hid** me in this sarcophagus, thinking no one would find me."

"I knew there was something **suspicious** about that **missing ship**," Geronimo mused.

"They thought they were clever," Creepella said. "But you were more clever, Father. You left us **CLUES** — pieces of your poem."

"I knew you would find them," Boris said.

"But **WHY** would Brad do such a thing?" Geronimo wondered.

"So he can **WIN** the contest," Boris said. "With me out of the picture, he can't lose."

"I suspect there's more to it than that, but we'll know soon enough," Creepella said. "But right now, we need to get you to that **contest!**"

"Um, do you think you can get me out of this thing first?" Boris asked.

Creepella frowned. "It's **SEALED** shut. But we'll find a way."

"Auntie, over here!" Shivereen called out.

"I found Professor Dubloon's **ship**!"

Creepella grinned. "**PERFECT!** Gerrykins, please load the sarcophagus onto the ship."

"But it's so **HEAVY**!" Geronimo protested, but of course it was no use. Creepella was already in the driver's seat. **HUFFING** and **PUFFING** again, he pushed the sarcophagus on board and then hopped in.

Creepella **SPED** back to the contest area, where Crystal Glamorosa was talking to the crowd.

"It seems as though Boris von Cacklefur has dropped out of the **contest**," she said. "According to the rules, that means that **Brad Balladeer** is the **winner**!"

Brad raised his arms in the air victoriously.

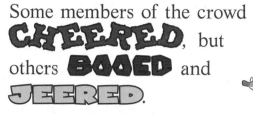

Some members of the crowd **CHEERED**, but others **BOOED** and **JEERED**.

"This has never happened before!" Professor Dubloon complained.

"And one of our judges is **MISSING**, too," added Professor Cleverpaws.

"Boris von Cacklefur is a **coward**," said Brad. "He ran away from a poetry contest in fourth grade. And that's just what he's done today!"

At that moment the pirate ship on wheels **BURST** onto the stage. The crowd gasped.

"EVERYONE LISTEN!"

Creepella cried.

Brad saw the sarcophagus and turned PALE.

"There's only one way you could know about what happened to my father in fourth grade, Brad," Creepella said. She pointed at him dramatically. "You are the son of CHESTER CHEATER!"

FRIGHT NIGHT IDOL!

The crowd went QUIET.

"We have proof," Creepella said, walking toward Brad. "Geronimo found your watch with the initials 'C.C.'"

Brad hung his head. "You are right," he said. "My real name is CHUMLEY CHEATER. Chester Cheater was my father."

The audience **gasped**.

"I *knew* he looked familiar!" Boris said from inside the sarcophagus.

"All I ever wanted to be was a great poet. I even changed my name," Brad said. "Being FRIGHT NIGHT IDOL has been my dream

come true, and I want to keep the title. But I learned that Boris von Cacklefur was competing this year, and my father said he was **impossible** to beat. So I mousenapped him!"

*"*Booooooooooooo!*"*

the audience jeered.

I'm a black belt!

Oops!

Panicked, Brad tried to run away, but Crystal **flipped** him over with a karate move.

The judges whispered to one another. Then Professor Dubloon announced, "Brad is **DISQUALIFIED**!"

"That means that Boris is the **winner**!" Crystal announced.

Where do you think you're going?

The Rattenbaum triplets tried to slink away, but Creepella spotted them.

"Don't go anywhere!" she said menacingly. "I'll deal with you soon."

There was still one problem — Boris was still trapped in the sarcophagus.

"How can I give him a cr🕳wn when he's in there?" Crystal asked.

Let's get you out of here!

Grandpa Frankenstein JUMPED out of his seat. "Let me take care of this — a baby mouse could do it!"

He took a strange contraption out of his bag and went to work. A few seconds later, Boris popped out of the sarcophagus.

Crystal put the crown on his head and announced,

"Your new Fright Night Idol is Boris von Cacklefur!"

Thunderous applause filled the arena.

"**Bravo!**" Creepella shouted, and her father shed a happy tear.

"And now, silence!" Crystal demanded. "Now let's hear our idol's most HORRIFYING poem!"

Boris began reciting.

The Phantom's Tale

Once upon a midnight scary,
I was feeding a ferocious canary,
When I heard a tapping, tapping on my door.
I called out, "What are you here for?"

It was the maid, and she was worried.
She said, "Please come, and we
must hurry!
Out to the graveyard — to the
graveyard we must go."
So I followed her, and I was
not slow.

Outside she showed me an
open grave.
And fright came over me like a wave.
Then we heard a stomping, stomping on
the ground.
It was followed by an eerie sound.

HEE HEE HEE HA HA HA

We turned and saw a ghostly rat.
He wore a coat and a sailor's hat.
And his arms were waving, waving in the air.
I steeled myself and asked, "Who goes there?"

"I was once Sailor Bill," the phantom said.
"I sailed the seas, but now I'm dead.
My heart was broken, broken by a lass.
And now I lie here under the grass."

"Your story is sad," I told poor Bill.
And then we all felt a terrible chill.
A wind came sweeping, sweeping over the vale.
And in a flash of light appeared a phantom female!

She said, "I broke your heart, Bill, that is true.
But you must know that I still love you."
Sailor Bill grabbed, grabbed his true love's paw.
Then they both disappeared. That is what I saw!

HEE HEE HEE

When Boris finished, the applause was so loud that the stands almost collapsed. Creepella, Shivereen, and Bitewing cheered harder than ever. Everyone loved "**THE PHANTOM'S TALE**"! Crystal invited everyone to the Fright Night party with food and dancing — everyone except for Brad and the Rattenbaum triplets, that is. They were forced to wash all of the **DISHES**!

"Today was the most deliciously DISMAL day ever, wasn't it, Gerrykins?" Creepella said happily.

Geronimo was too tired to argue with her.

"But you know what the **best** thing is?" Creepella went on.

"NOW I HAVE LOTS OF MATERIAL FOR A NEW SCARY BOOK!"

THE END

An Award for Creepella!

I'm still helping out with that encyclopedia, but I decided to take a break from Mysterious Valley for a while. That place gives me the **shivers!**

So I went back to New Mouse City and soon published Creepella's book. It became a bestseller on the very first day!

Benjamin finished his report on ancient Greece, and he got an **A+**. So we decided to go out and **CELEBRATE** at the ice cream parlor. As we were eating our sundaes with delicious Swiss **CHEESE** sauce, Bitewing flew into the parlor.

"**URGENT** telegram for Geronimo Stilton!" the bat announced.

"Is it from Creepella?" Benjamin asked.

"It's from the Academy of Shivery Arts," I said as I read it. "She's getting an award for

They want me to present the award to her."

"Will you go?" asked my nephew.

"He will if he knows what's good for him!" **Bitewing** said threateningly.

I sighed. Mysterious Valley is so bizarre, and I wasn't in a hurry to go back there. But Creepella is my friend, and I was thrilled that she was getting an award. She deserved it. I could already imagine what I'd say in my speech.

"It's an honor for me to give this award to Creepella von Cacklefur! Nobody can write a **SCARY** book better than she can! And I'm sure that she'll soon amaze us with another thrilling **BESTSELLER!**"

She's the best!

If you liked this book, be sure to check out my other adventures!

#1 THE THIRTEEN GHOSTS

#2 MEET ME IN HORRORWOOD

#3 GHOST PIRATE TREASURE

#4 RETURN OF THE VAMPIRE

#5 FRIGHT NIGHT

#19 My Name Is Stilton, Geronimo Stilton

#20 Surf's Up, Geronimo!

#21 The Wild, Wild West

#22 The Secret of Cacklefur Castle

A Christmas Tale

#23 Valentine's Day Disaster

#24 Field Trip to Niagara Falls

#25 The Search for Sunken Treasure

#26 The Mummy with No Name

#27 The Christmas Toy Factory

#28 Wedding Crasher

#29 Down and Out Down Under

#30 The Mouse Island Marathon

#31 The Mysterious Cheese Thief

Christmas Catastrophe

#32 Valley of the Giant Skeletons

#33 Geronimo and the Gold Medal Mystery

#34 Geronimo Stilton, Secret Agent

#35 A Very Merry Christmas

#36 Geronimo's Valentine

#37 The Race Across America

#38 A Fabumouse School Adventure

#39 Singing Sensation

#40 The Karate Mouse

#41 Mighty Mount Kilimanjaro

#42 The Peculiar Pumpkin Thief

#43 I'm Not a Supermouse!

#44 The Giant Diamond Robbery

#45 Save the White Whale!

#46 The Haunted Castle

#47 Run for the Hills, Geronimo!

#48 The Mystery in Venice

#49 The Way of the Samurai

#50 This Hotel Is Haunted!

#51 The Enormouse Pearl Heist

#52 Mouse in Space!

#53 Rumble in the Jungle

#54 Get into Gear, Stilton!

Up next:

#55 The Golden Statue Plot

Be sure to check out these exciting Thea Sisters adventures!

Thea Stilton and the Dragon's Code

Thea Stilton and the Mountain of Fire

Thea Stilton and the Ghost of the Shipwreck

Thea Stilton and the Secret City

Thea Stilton and the Mystery in Paris

Thea Stilton and the Cherry Blossom Adventure

Thea Stilton and the Star Castaways

Thea Stilton: Big Trouble in the Big Apple

Thea Stilton and the Ice Treasure

Thea Stilton and the Secret of the Old Castle

Thea Stilton and the Blue Scarab Hunt

Thea Stilton and the Prince's Emerald

Thea Stilton and the Mystery on the Orient Express

Thea Stilton and the Dancing Shadows

Thea Stilton and the Legend of the Fire Flowers

Thea Stilton and the Spanish Dance Mission

1. Mountains of the Mangy Yeti
2. Cacklefur Castle
3. Angry Walnut Tree
4. Rattenbaum Mansion
5. Rancidrat River
6. Bridge of Shaky Steps
7. Squeakspeare Mansion
8. Slimy Swamp
9. Ogre Highway
10. Gloomeria
11. Shivery Arts Academy
12. Horrorwood Studios

CACKLEFUR CASTLE

1. Oozing moat

2. Drawbridge

3. Grand entrance

4. Moldy basement

5. Patio, with a view of the moat

6. Dusty library

7. Room for unwanted guests

8. Mummy room

9. Watchtower

10. Creaking staircase

11. Banquet room

12. Garage (for antique hearses)

13. Bewitched tower

14. Garden of carnivorous plants

15. Stinky kitchen

16. Crocodile pool and piranha tank

17. Creepella's room

18. Tower of musky tarantulas

19. Bitewing's tower (with antique contraptions)

DEAR MOUSE FRIENDS, GOOD-BYE UNTIL THE NEXT BOOK!